Finding Chocolate Alleys!

To Henry
Deborah Gould

By Deborah Gould
Illustrated by Judith Rush

For information about this title or to order other books and/
or electronic media, contact the publisher:

978-1-7334359-2-5   Hardcover ISBN
978-1-7334359-0-1   Softcover ISBN
978-1-7334359-1-8   eBook ISBN

322 Cocoa Publishing
P.O. Box 4262
Lancaster, PA 17604

www.cocoa-girl.com

Cover and Interior design: 1106 Design

To Eleanor and Joe,
for making it
possible,
to Tara and Melissa,
Bennett, Finn and
Emma
to explore and find
your joy,
to Tom for being there

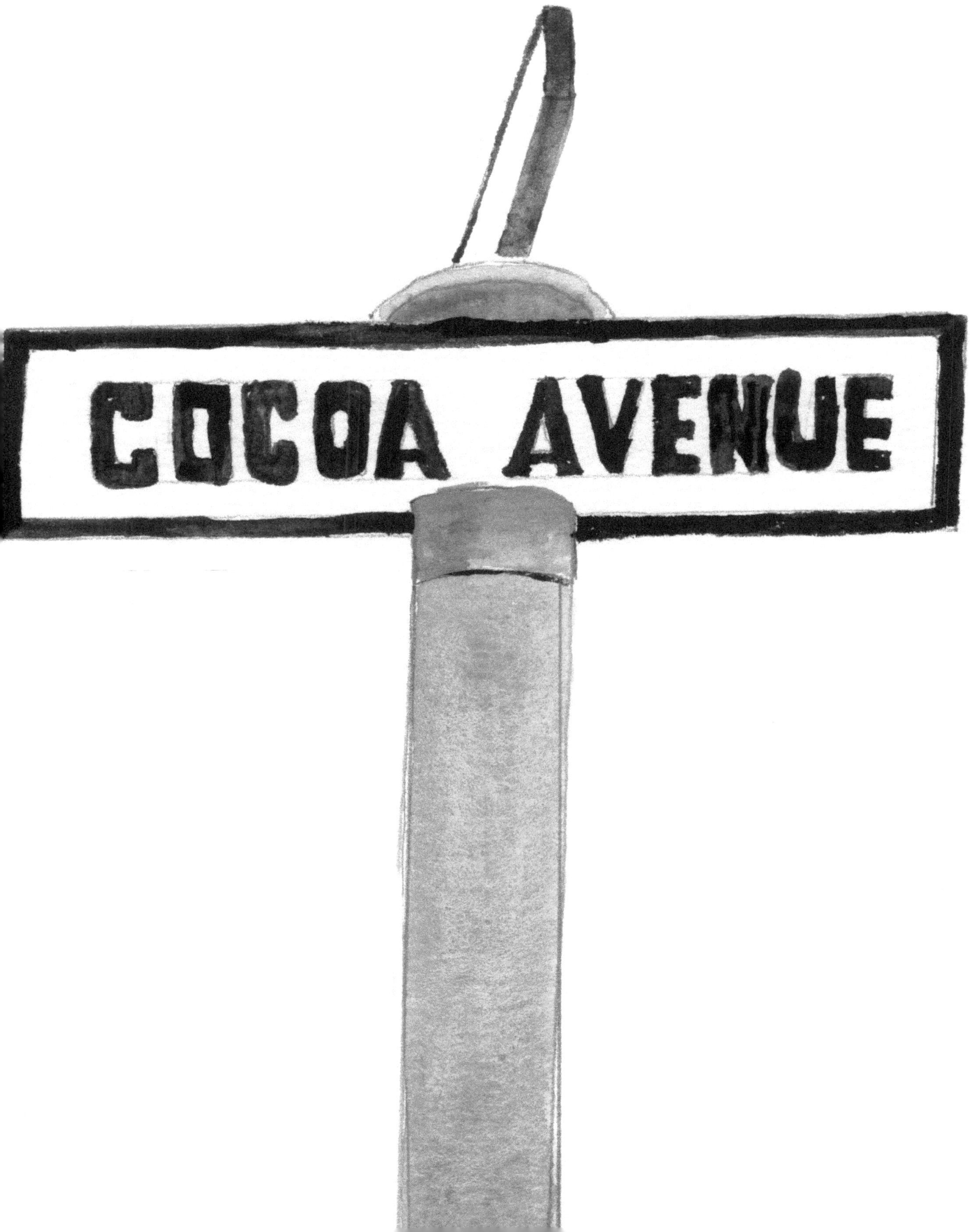
COCOA AVENUE

Annelisa hurried up the steps onto the wide porch that stretched across the front of her white house.

This day felt warmer, the sky was bluer and the grass was greener.
She saw the front door and could not wait
to run out the back door!

She felt excited for two reasons —
the last day of third grade had ended,
and the first day of summer vacation had begun!

Annelisa Gold thought about spending the whole summer playing in the backyard at her house on Cocoa Avenue.

Her big brown eyes opened wide,
she pushed her tangled hair away from her freckled face
...and walked in the front door.

She thought about playing with her sister, Jo.

The sisters played in the backyard, lined with a wire fence
where a sidewalk led to a white wooden garage.

Flowers and bushes lined the back fence,
and an apple tree canopied the middle of the yard.

Annelisa and Jo liked to sit under the tree
and play with dolls
and dress their paper dolls.

She also planned to play with her box turtle who lived in the backyard.
Boxy, the turtle, lived in a large cardboard box –
lined with grass.

He ate pieces of tomato and small bugs.
Annelisa would set Boxy down to wander around the yard.

On that summer day, she burst out the back door to get Boxy.
He was not in the box!
Annelisa searched the fenced yard. Was he hiding? Annelisa crawled
along the line of bushes and lay on her belly to look under the spreading
bushes. She walked up and down the grass,
separating blades of grass with her feet.

She
looked
everywhere!

Inside the garage were
the family car,

her father's green lawnmower

and her new bicycle.

Annelisa's mother suggested that she walk or ride up the alley to look
for him.
Could Boxy have squeezed through the wire fence?

Annelisa sadly walked toward the garage
and opened the garage door, which faced the alley.
Inside, Annelisa's bicycle leaned on a wall.

It was a red two-wheeler with a wire basket and a bell on the
handlebar.

Riding her red bike up the
alley would be more fun than walking.

She pushed the kickstand up,
sat on the brown leather seat,
and headed up the alley.

Annelisa smiled. She felt excited,
because it was the first time
she was riding a bike on her own.

She rode her bike in the alleys
behind
and
beyond her house
on Cocoa Avenue, searching for her turtle.

Alleys stretched for blocks or turned into other alleys.
This small town was a maze of connected alleys.
As Annelisa rode, she would zoom fast or pedal so slowly her bike stood still.
She did not find her turtle, but she was free to explore on her own!

As she pedaled past rows of garages lining each alley,
Annelisa saw and heard people in their yards.
Behind the closed garage doors were backyards
full of trees, bushes, vegetable and flower gardens, and grassy lawns
that led to a house on a street.

Annelisa saw people hanging laundry on clotheslines,
cutting grass, picking flowers, watering and tending to gardens.
She saw children and heard laughter
as they climbed trees
or played tag.

Annelisa was ready to ride into the middle of the town.

In the middle of the small town stood a large stone factory
where
chocolate
candy
was made.

Annelisa had often walked by that factory,
looking at the tangled ivy vines
climbing up the gray stone walls.

She rode her bike in a world of turns through alleys, and sometimes
the alleys led to streets.
Annelisa turned off a street corner at Cocoa Avenue and rode onto
Chocolate Avenue, the main street.
Her bike hugged the street as she pedaled slowly close to the factory.

The factory looked like a castle.

It reached to the sky and filled a whole city block.
The air was warm with moisture and
tiny puddles of dew had formed on the grass.

On that breezy day, Annelisa took a deep breath to smell... chocolate!

Chocolate filled her nose!
Gooey, rich, sweet chocolate air swirled around everywhere.
The chocolate air flowed out of the chocolate factory and
floated
through the town that day and on many summer days.
Chocolate air
filled the alleyways to the garage roofs
with chocolate sauce.

Annelisa smiled when she glided her
bike through all the

Chocolate Alleys.

When she smelled chocolate air,
she knew that she was in a

chocolate alley!

Annelisa took a bite of the air.

She rode her bike fast, so the chocolate air whipped through her tangled hair.

Annelisa popped the chocolate air in her mouth and felt the sweet chocolate melt...slowly...licking her lips to taste each chocolate puddle.

She lived in a small town where chocolate air spread everywhere, even into alleys!

Most summer days chocolate air swirled
around Annelisa.
Some days the chocolate air was hiding and
she could <u>not</u> smell it. Annelisa would run
outside in the morning,
put her nose up to the sky,
close her eyes,
and take a deep whiff.

In an instant, Annelisa knew
if the moist chocolate air was hiding or not.

Summer days were spent riding her bike in the *Chocolate Alleys* savoring the smell of chocolate.

Annelisa never found her turtle.

She did find freedom on her red bike, whizzing past backyards or coasting into a turn that led from one alley to the next.

She explored alleys and streets and experienced more than she had imagined.

Annelisa Gold was
lucky to be growing up
in a town where she
could find
**Chocolate
Alleys!**

Words to Know

Alley – narrow street behind houses

Alleyway – another word for alley

Canopied – cover an area

Clothesline – a wire between two poles on which washed clothes are hung to dry

Freckled – small patch of light brown color on skin

Gooey – soft and sticky

Maze – network or paths like a puzzle where one has to find a way

Stretched – reach as far as possible in a direction

Swirled – move in a twisting pattern

Tangled – twisted together

Whiff – smell for a short time

Whipped air – softly mixed

Whizzing – move fast through the air

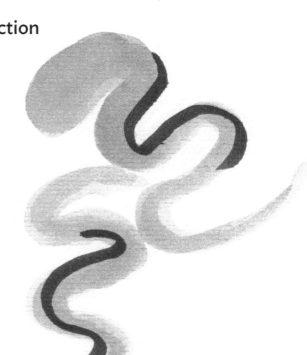

Author

Deborah Gould is an educator and grandmother
who wants to inspire children to explore and
learn about their world. There is endless joy in
searching yards and neighborhoods, while using
your senses to see, smell, hear, taste and touch as
you explore. She grew up in a town with chocolate
in the air and now lives in Lancaster, Pa.

Illustrator

Judith Rush is an artist and grandmother who
understands the joys of growing up. She brings
stories to life with her artistic depictions of children's
lives. She now lives in Winston Salem, NC.

After you read about finding 'chocolate alleys',
    You will create your own stories.

You can find adventure wherever you live.
    Annelisa searched for her turtle
    and found freedom zooming on a bike...
    through an alley that led to a
    castle
    surrounded by
    chocolate air.

What do you want to look for?
What will you find?

It's Your Turn to be an Author!
Write Your Story Here...

It's Your Turn to be an Illustrator!
Draw Pictures for Your Story Here...

CPSIA information can be obtained
at www.ICGtesting.com
Printed in the USA
BVHW022344170422
634469BV00003B/75

9 781733 435901